MW00974945

This book belongs to:

_____

DISNEY
PRINCESS

THE Princess AND THE Frog

The Story of Tiana

Disney PRINCESS

THE
Princess
AND THE
Frog

The Story of Tiana

Disney PRESS
Los Angeles • New York

Copyright © 2016 Disney Enterprises, Inc. All rights reserved.

Published by Disney Press, an imprint of Disney Book Group. No part of this book may
be reproduced or transmitted in any form or by any means, electronic or mechanical,
including photocopying, recording, or by any information storage and retrieval system,
without written permission from the publisher. For information address Disney Press,
1101 Flower Street, Glendale, California 91201.

Printed in the United States of America
First Hardcover Edition, January 2016
1 3 5 7 9 10 8 6 4 2

Library of Congress Control Number: 2015947453
FAC-038091-15324
ISBN 978-1-4847-6729-0

SUSTAINABLE
FORESTRY   Certified Sourcing
INITIATIVE   www.sfiprogram.org
SFI-00993
This Label Applies to Text Stock Only

disneybooks.com

*You can do anything you put
your mind to . . .*

IN A STATELY MANSION IN A LOVELY neighborhood in New Orleans, two young girls named Tiana and Charlotte shared an unlikely friendship. While Charlotte believed in wishing with all her heart, Tiana knew that wishing would help her only if she worked hard to pursue her dreams.

One night, Tiana's mother, Eudora, the best seamstress in town, asked the girls what they thought of the story of the prince who had been turned into a frog.

"There is no way in this whole wide world I would ever, ever, ever—I mean never—kiss a frog!" Tiana said.

"I would kiss a hundred frogs if I could marry a prince and be a princess!" Charlotte exclaimed.

After returning to her cozy home, Tiana helped her father, James, prepare a pot of gumbo for dinner. Just like James, the little girl loved to cook.

Tiana tasted it, added one more ingredient, then said, "I think it's done!"

"Well, sweetheart, this is the BEST gumbo I've ever tasted!" James said. "A gift this special's just got to be shared."

Tiana and her parents invited all the neighbors to share the good food. The night air was filled with the sounds of clinking spoons, conversation, and laughter.

"You see," said Tiana's father, "food brings folks together." He knew family and friends were what was really important.

Tiana and her father dreamed of opening a restaurant someday. So that night, her parents encouraged her to wish on the Evening Star.

"But remember," added James, "you've got to help it along with some hard work of your own."

The years went by and Tiana grew up. James passed
away, but Tiana was still determined to make their
restaurant dream come true. To do that, she waited
tables and saved every spare penny she could.
She rarely had time for fun.

One morning, everyone gathered for the arrival of the handsome Prince Naveen of Maldonia. As he disembarked, the prince immediately started playing jazz music!

His poor valet, Lawrence, stumbled along behind, toting the prince's luggage.

Charlotte and her father, "Big Daddy" LaBouff, arrived for breakfast at Duke's, where Tiana was working. "Oh, Tia!" Charlotte said. "Did you hear? Prince Naveen of Maldonia is coming to New Orleans, and Big Daddy invited him to our masquerade ball tonight! I'm going to need about five hundred of your man-catching beignets."

Thanks to Charlotte's beignet order, Tiana had finally saved enough money to make an offer on the old sugar mill. She met with Mr. Fenner and his brother, the real estate brokers, and then watched happily as the men drove away to prepare the paperwork.

"Table for one, please!" came a voice from behind Tiana. It was her mother, Eudora, holding James's old gumbo pot as a gift.

"I've gotta make sure all Daddy's hard work means something," Tiana said. She saw a bright future for the restaurant, but Eudora saw a lot of work.

"Tiana, your daddy may not have gotten the place he always wanted, but he had something better," Eudora said. "He had love. And that's all I want for you, sweetheart."

Meanwhile, Lawrence reminded Prince Naveen that he was there to marry a rich young lady—or get a job! Just then, Dr. Facilier approached.

Peering at the prince's hand, Facilier proclaimed, "I'd wager I'm in the company of visiting royalty!"

"Lawrence, this remarkable gentleman has just read my palm," the prince said.

"Or this morning's newspaper," Lawrence muttered. He had spotted the paper announcing Naveen's arrival in Facilier's pocket.

But soon the evil Dr. Facilier convinced the men he could give them their hearts' desires—if they followed him to his lair.

Cautious at first, Naveen and Lawrence eventually found themselves shaking hands with Facilier to seal the deal. Instantly, the room came alive with magic. The spell had been cast!

Meanwhile, the masquerade ball at the LaBouff estate was well under way. But Charlotte's prince hadn't come.

"It's just not fair! I never get anything I wish for!" Charlotte complained to Tiana. She gazed up at the Evening Star and pleaded: "Please, please, please—"

Then Charlotte's wish came true! Prince Naveen made his grand entrance! Within moments, Charlotte was dancing with her prince.

While Charlotte danced, Tiana spotted the Fenner brothers. They informed her they had another buyer for the sugar mill—and she needed to come up with more cash!

Tiana was crushed. She tried to stop the Fenner brothers from walking away on their deal but toppled into her beignets instead.

She borrowed a clean dress from Charlotte and stepped onto the balcony.

"I cannot believe I'm doing this," she said as she made a wish on the Evening Star for her restaurant. She opened her eyes—and spotted a frog!

"I reckon you want a kiss?" Tiana joked.

"Kissing would be nice, yes?" the frog replied.

Tiana shrieked and ran back into Charlotte's bedroom, hurling anything she could find at the creature.

"Please allow me to introduce myself," he said. "I am Prince Naveen of Maldonia."

Tiana was confused. "If you're the prince, then who was that waltzing with Lottie on the dance floor?"

A Handsome Prince!

They were married
And lived happily
ever after.

Naveen didn't know. Thinking Tiana was a princess who could break the spell, he insisted that her kiss would transform him back into a human. He even offered her a reward.

Tiana felt sorry for the little frog. Plus the reward would help her get her restaurant. So she leaned in, closed her eyes . . . and kissed him. *POOF!*

"Aaiieeeeee!" Tiana screamed.

Now both Tiana and Naveen were frogs! Frantic, they catapulted out the window and onto the dance floor below. "Get those frogs!" Big Daddy commanded Charlotte's dog. Naveen grabbed some balloons and held on to Tiana. "Going up!" he shouted, and they floated into the sky.

In the LaBouffs' guest quarters, Dr. Facilier cornered the "prince." The doctor had used his magic to change Prince Naveen into a frog and Lawrence into Prince Naveen!

Facilier and Lawrence had a plan for Lawrence to marry Charlotte and claim her father's fortune. But the magic to keep Lawrence looking like the prince required frog's blood trapped in a talisman—and Lawrence had let the frog escape!

Meanwhile, Tiana and Naveen had landed in the bayou, bickering about why the kiss hadn't worked. But soon dangerous alligators surrounded the two frogs! Tiana escaped into a hollow tree, but Naveen was stuck below.

"Help me get out of this swamp, and once I marry Charlotte, I shall get you your restaurant," he promised.

Tiana pulled him to safety.

Now that they were safe, Tiana steered a makeshift boat while Naveen relaxed on it. But when a huge alligator surfaced, both frogs froze in terror!

Fortunately, Louis was a friendly gator who simply wanted to talk about music! He and Naveen jabbered about jazz, including Louis's prized trumpet.

When Louis learned the frogs wanted to turn human again, he had an idea: "Mama Odie! She's got magic."

As Lawrence lunched with Charlotte, the magic in the talisman began to run out! Lawrence's ears bulged, his backside expanded, and his nose ballooned. He rushed to propose to her before the magic disappeared completely!

Charlotte was too excited to notice the change. "Yes! I most definitely will marry you!" she exclaimed.

Back in the bayou, the group traveled to Mama Odie and met a firefly called Ray.

When Ray heard where the frogs were headed, he offered to guide them. With a whistle, he summoned his family—a shimmering chain of fireflies—to light the way.

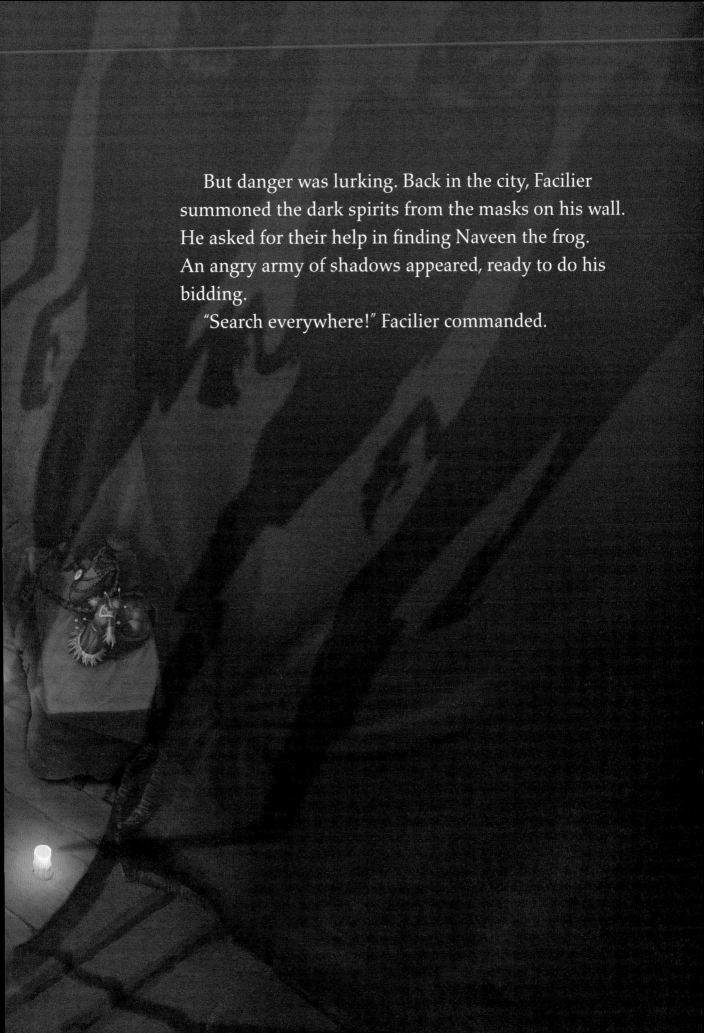

But danger was lurking. Back in the city, Facilier
summoned the dark spirits from the masks on his wall.
He asked for their help in finding Naveen the frog.
An angry army of shadows appeared, ready to do his
bidding.

"Search everywhere!" Facilier commanded.

Meanwhile, in the soft light of the evening, Ray told Tiana about his true love, Evangeline. "She's the most prettiest firefly that ever did glow," he said.

"Just do not settle down so quickly," Naveen said.

Tiana rolled her eyes and followed Ray away from the water and through the brush while Louis followed her, trying to escape the pricker bushes.

WHOOSH! A net swooped down and scooped up Naveen. Three hunters were out to capture frogs!

Louis ran for cover, but Ray flew to the rescue. "A bug's got to do what a bug's got to do!" he cried as he shot straight up one hunter's nose.

Naveen escaped, but Tiana landed in a cage.

As soon as Naveen saw Tiana with the hunters, he raced to help her.
Together, they outwitted the men.

"These two ain't like no frogs I ever seen!" one man exclaimed.

"And we talk, too!" Tiana said.

Laughing, Tiana and Naveen hopped into the trees, happy to be working
together.

As Ray helped Louis, who was covered in prickers,
Tiana started cooking. She told Naveen to mince some
mushrooms, but he didn't know how.

"I have never done anything like this before," he said.

Tiana was happy to teach Naveen. Soon the frogs
were laughing as they worked.

After supper, with their bellies full, the friends looked up at the night sky.

"There she is—the sweetest firefly in all creation," Ray said. Tiana looked up and realized that Ray was speaking of the Evening Star, not a firefly!

While Louis played a song on his trumpet, Naveen and Tiana danced together to the music.

Then, all at once, dark shadows sent by Dr. Facilier descended on the
bayou, grabbing Naveen. Tiana screamed and tried to hold on to her friend.
Even Louis and little Ray helped, but the shadows were too powerful.

FOOM! A blinding light vaporized the shadows. Mama Odie had arrived just in time to save Naveen.

"Not bad for a 197-year-old blind lady!" she exclaimed.

She led them inside her home, an old shrimp boat nestled in a tree. Tiana tried to explain why they had come, but Mama Odie already knew.

The old magic woman stirred a bathtub full of gumbo and asked Tiana,
"Now, y'all figure out what you need?"

"We need to be human," Tiana replied.

"Y'all want to be human, but you're blind to what you need!" Mama
Odie said, knowing the frogs would have to learn things the hard way.

At last Mama Odie conjured an image of Charlotte and her father in the tub of gumbo. Big Daddy was to be king of Mardi Gras, which made Charlotte a princess. If Naveen kissed Charlotte before midnight, he and Tiana would both be human again.

There was no time to lose! The friends hopped aboard a riverboat of Mardi Gras revelers and headed back to New Orleans.

On the boat, Naveen realized how much he loved Tiana. Just as he was about to propose, Tiana spotted the sugar mill. "There it is!" she exclaimed. But Naveen did not have the money to help her get her restaurant by the next day's deadline. Feeling sad about letting Tiana down, he walked away alone.

When Naveen was by himself, the shadows
pounced! They brought him back to Dr. Facilier, who
used the refilled talisman to turn Lawrence back into
the handsome prince.

Facilier locked Naveen inside a small chest and
hurried off.

At the dock, Ray blurted Naveen's secret to Tiana. "He's not going to marry Charlotte. He's in love with you!"

Tiana felt the same way! But when she got to the Mardi Gras parade, she spotted the wedding cake float—with Charlotte and Prince Naveen getting married on top of it.

Thinking Naveen did not love her anymore, Tiana turned away.

But Ray knew Naveen wouldn't marry anyone else! He flew up to the float, found the real Naveen inside the locked chest, and set him free.

As Charlotte and her impostor groom were about to say "I do," the frog prince jumped onto Lawrence and grabbed the talisman from his neck.

Lawrence and Naveen toppled off the float and raced into a nearby building.

"Lawrence, why are you doing this?" Naveen asked. As Facilier approached, the frog prince shot out his tongue, grabbed the talisman, and tossed it to Ray, who caught it and flew away.

"Stay out of sight," Facilier said to Lawrence, who looked like himself again. Then the doctor summoned the shadows to hunt down Ray.

In the cemetery, Ray spotted Tiana and tossed the talisman to her, telling her to run while he battled the shadows with his firefly light. But Facilier smacked the bug to the ground and stepped on him.

The doctor caught up with Tiana. She threatened to smash the talisman, destroying Facilier's evil magic. But Facilier blew a puff of magic dust, giving her a vision. . . .

Tiana magically saw herself standing in her dream restaurant. "All you got to do to make this a reality is hand over that little ol' talisman of mine," Facilier said. He knew how important the restaurant was to her and her daddy.

"Don't forget your poor daddy," Facilier added.

Remembering her father, Tiana cried out, "He never lost sight of what was really important. And neither will I!"

She threw the talisman to the ground, smashing it.

All at once, the vision was gone, and the shadows closed in on Dr. Facilier. Tiana watched in terror. Soon the shadows disappeared among the gravestones, and all that was left of Dr. Facilier was his black top hat.

Tiana found Naveen talking to Charlotte.

"If I kiss you before midnight, you and Tiana will turn human again?" Charlotte asked Naveen. "And then we gonna get ourselves married and live happily ever after! The end!"

"But remember," Naveen said. "You must give Tiana all the money she requires for her restaurant."

"Wait!" Tiana shouted. Naveen turned to her. "My dream wouldn't be complete without you in it."

Charlotte knew her friend was in love. She looked at Tiana and said, "I'll kiss him for you, honey. No marriage required!" But her kiss was too late. The clock struck midnight, and Charlotte was no longer the Mardi Gras princess.

Though Tiana and Naveen were still frogs, they had found true love.

Then Louis ran to them and placed an injured Ray on a feather.

Naveen held Tiana as he told Ray, "We're staying together."

"I like that very much," Ray said. "Evangeline likes that, too." Then his little light flickered out for the last time.

Later, in the bayou, Tiana and Naveen joined Louis to bid their loyal friend Ray good-bye forever. When Ray's friends lifted their eyes skyward, they saw the dazzling Evening Star—and, next to it, another bright star no one had ever seen before.

Ray had been right. True love always finds a way.

In the morning, Tiana and Naveen got married.

As Naveen kissed his new wife, something magical happened. He and Tiana turned back into humans! The frog prince had finally kissed a true princess.

"Once you became my wife, that made you . . ." Naveen began.

"A princess," Tiana said. "You just kissed a princess!"

Tiana and Naveen had a second wedding to share their joy with their human friends and family.

Eudora was delighted to see her daughter happy—and the prince's parents were thrilled to see that their son had turned into a responsible and caring young man. He even worked hard with Tiana to fix up the sugar mill.

At long last, Tiana opened her restaurant, Tiana's Palace. Louis led swinging music, and the food was the best around.

But what made Tiana's Palace special was the way it brought folks together.

Finally, Tiana had everything she wanted—and all she needed.

To be continued . . .